REAL WORLD MATH

Extreme SPORTS

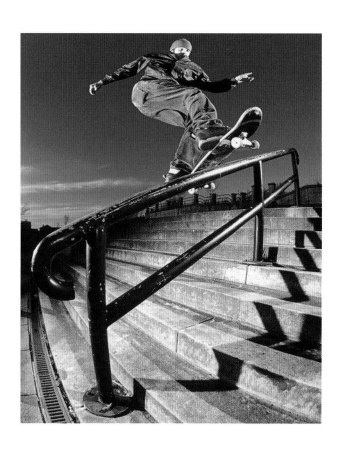

by Wendy Clemson, David Clemson, Oli Cundale, Laura Berry, and Matt King

An Hachette UK Company
www.hachette.co.uk
First published in the USA in 2013 by
TickTock, an imprint of Octopus Publishing Group Ltd
Endeavour House,189 Shaftesbury Avenue, London WC2H 8JY
www.octopusbooks.co.uk
www.octopusbooksusa.com

Copyright © Octopus Publishing Group Ltd 2013

Distributed in the US by
Hachette Book Group USA
237 Park Avenue, New York NY 10017, USA

Distributed in Canada by
Canadian Manda Group
165 Dufferin Street, Toronto, Ontario, Canada M6K 3H6

All rights reserved. No part of this work may be reproduced or utilized in any form or by any means,
electronic or mechanical, including photocopying, recording, or by any information storage and retrieval system,
without the prior written permission of the publisher.

With thanks to our consultants: Jenni Back and Liz Pumfrey from the NRICH Project,
Cambridge University, and to Kerry Johnson and Debra Voege.

ISBN 978 1 84898 205 5

Printed and bound in China

10 9 8 7 6 5 4 3 2 1

WENDY CLEMSON

Wendy is experienced in working with and for children, and has been writing full-time since 1989. Her publications, which now exceed one hundred, have been written for children and sometimes their parents and teachers. In her many math books, the aim is always to present the reader with challenges that are fun.

DAVID CLEMSON

David has wide-ranging experience as a writer and educationalist. His publications list is prodigious. In collaboration with Wendy, David has worked on many math books for children. He is fascinated by math and logic puzzles and is eager for the reader to enjoy them, too.

WARNING

This book is not intended to be a training manual for the sports of skateboarding, snowboarding, or inline skating. If you would like to try any of the sports featured in this book, wear the correct protective clothing and take some lessons from a professional instructor before attempting tricks on a skateboard, snowboard, or pair of skates.

The extreme tricks and stunts featured in this book have been performed by professional, highly experienced sportsmen and sportswomen. Read about the tricks and stunts, say, "WOW," but under no circumstances try them yourself! If you do, don't blame us – **WE TOLD YOU NOT TO TRY THEM!**
(Neither the publisher nor the authors shall be liable for any bodily harm or damage to property whatsoever that may be caused or sustained as a result of conducting any of the activities featured in this book.)

CONTENTS

MATH SKILLS COVERED IN THIS BOOK:

CALCULATIONS:
Throughout this book there are opportunities to practice **addition, subtraction, multiplication,** and **division** using both mental calculation strategies and pencil and paper methods.

NUMBERS AND THE NUMBER SYSTEM:
- COMPARING NUMBERS: pg. 7
- DECIMALS: pgs. 10, 26
- FRACTIONS: pgs. 18, 26
- NEGATIVE NUMBERS (on a number line/temperature scale): pgs. 26, 27
- ORDERING NUMBERS: pgs. 10, 26
- ROUNDING: pg. 7

SOLVING "REAL LIFE" PROBLEMS:
- CHOOSING THE OPERATION: pgs. 17, 18, 24
- MONEY: pg. 24
- TIME: pgs. 15, 17, 19

HANDLING DATA:
- BAR GRAPHS: pgs. 6, 13
- PICTOGRAPHS: pg. 14
- TALLY CHARTS: pg. 25
- USING TABLES/CHARTS/DIAGRAMS: pgs. 10, 12
- VENN DIAGRAMS: pg. 22

MEASURES:
- AREA: pg. 23
- PERIMETER: pg. 23
- RELATIONSHIPS BETWEEN UNITS OF MEASUREMENT: pgs. 11, 26
- SCALES (reading from a scale): pg. 27
- USING MEASUREMENTS: pgs. 7, 11, 13, 18, 19, 20
- VOCABULARY (time): pgs. 15, 17, 19

SHAPE AND SPACE:
- 2-D SHAPES: pg. 22
- ANGLES: pgs. 8, 9
- LINE SYMMETRY: pg. 21

Supports math standards for grades 4–6

HOW TO USE THIS BOOK

Math is important in the lives of people everywhere. We use math when we play a game, ride a bike, go shopping – in fact, all the time! Everyone uses math when they take part in sports. You may not realize it, but extreme sportsmen and sportswomen use math to perform tricks and win competitions! With this book you will get the chance to try lots of exciting math activities using real life data and facts about extreme sports. Practice your math skills and experience the thrill of what it's really like to be a top extreme athlete.

This exciting math book is very easy to use – check out what's inside!

Fun-to-read information about skateboarding, inline skating, and snowboarding.

SNOWBOARDING with Laura

Laura says, "Snowboarding is exciting, fun, and gives me a buzz! I get the chance to travel all over the world, meet new people, and make new friends. As long as everybody is having fun, snowboarders of all abilities will ride together, offering each other encouragement and helping each other progress and improve. I personally love to ride anywhere that has *big air jumps*, *superpipes* and technical rails. Snowboarding competitions can take place on mountains, at indoor snow slopes, and on dry slopes. There are lots of different types of snowboarding competitions – *Pipe*, *Big Air*, *Snowboarder-cross* and *Slopestyle*."

MATH ACTIVITIES

Look for the
GO FOR IT! CLIPBOARDS.
You will find real life math activities and questions.

To answer some of the questions, you will need to collect data from a DATA BOX. Sometimes, you will need to collect facts and data from the text or from charts and diagrams.

Be prepared! You will need a pen or pencil and a notebook to figure out the answers.

GO FOR IT!

It is the final of a *halfpipe competition*. **Halfpipes** are like a giant pipe that has been cut in half. They are made of snow. Snowboarders ride down the pipe performing tricks. They are awarded points out of 10 in four categories. The rider with the highest total score is the winner.

In the DATA BOX you will see the scores for six halfpipe finalists.

1) Who got the lowest total score?
2) Who did better than Rob in both **amplitude** and overall impression?
3) Who got the same score as Zak?
4) How many people had total scores that were odd numbers? What were their scores?
5) Who got the highest score and won the halfpipe competition?

(You will find TIPS to help you with these questions on page 28.)

A snowboarding halfpipe

The lip

SNOWBOARDING FACT

In *snowboarder-cross*, riders race downhill around and over obstacles in groups of six. Courses can be nearly two-thirds of a mile in length. The fastest rider in each group goes through to a final. The first rider to the bottom in the final wins gold! In *slopestyle*, competitors take three runs down a course filled with rails, jumps, and quarterpipes.

Fun-to-read facts about EXTREME sports.

DATA BOX

If you see one of these boxes, there will be important data inside that will help you with the math activities.

HAVE FUN, BUT STAY SAFE!

It's easy for extreme athletes to hurt themselves if they don't follow these important safety rules:

- Wear a helmet at all times and make sure it fits snugly.
- Wear knee pads, elbow pads, and gloves or wrist guards.
- Take some lessons – a qualified instructor will make sure you know what you are doing!
- Never try a trick that is above your level – start small and build up slowly.
- Always try these sports with friends. It's more fun, and if one of you gets injured, someone can go for help.

MATH ACTIVITIES

Feeling confident?
Try these extra
CHALLENGE QUESTIONS.

DATA BOX HALFPIPE SCORES (POINTS OUT OF 40)

NAME	STANDARD AIRS	ROTATIONS	AMPLITUDE	OVERALL IMPRESSION
Lyn	5	9	8	4
Rob	8	8	7	8
Ahmed	6	9	6	9
Laura	9	8	8	7
Zak	7	7	8	9
Alli	8	5	5	5

- *STANDARD AIRS*: Tricks and movements such as grabs.
- *ROTATIONS* (spins and flips): 180°, 360° (a full spin), 540°, 720°, 900°, 1080°, 1260°.
- *AMPLITUDE*: The height the rider reaches above the lip of the pipe.
- *OVERALL IMPRESSION*: Style, level of difficulty of tricks, creativity, and landings.

SNOWBOARDING FACT

The highest *Big air* ever achieved was 30 feet above the lip of the halfpipe. The biggest spin that has ever been done on a jump, is a *1260* (that's 1,260 **degrees** – three and half full spins while in the air).

IF YOU NEED HELP...

TIPS FOR MATH SUCCESS

On pages 28–29 you will find lots of tips to help you with your math work.

ANSWERS

Turn to pages 30–31 to check your answers.
(Try all the activities and questions before you take a look at the answers.)

GLOSSARY

On page 32 there is a glossary of extreme sports words and a glossary of math words. The glossary words appear **in bold** in the text.

CHALLENGE QUESTIONS

In *Big Air competitions*, riders perform big jumps.
They launch themselves out of a halfpipe and pull a trick.
Competitors are marked on height, style, and number of rotations.

This graph shows the amplitude (height) of some snowboarders' *big air jumps*.

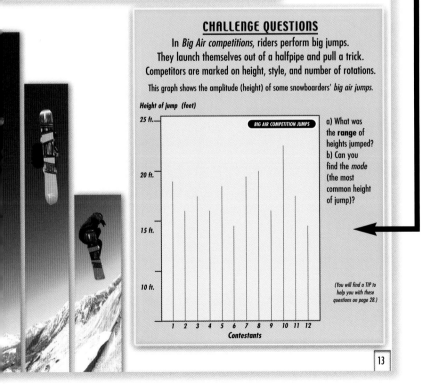

Height of jump (feet)

BIG AIR COMPETITION JUMPS

25 ft.
20 ft.
15 ft.
10 ft.

1 2 3 4 5 6 7 8 9 10 11 12
Contestants

a) What was the **range** of heights jumped?
b) Can you find the *mode* (the most common height of jump)?

(You will find a TIP to help you with these questions on page 28.)

13

5

Skateboarding, inline skating, and snowboarding are extreme sports. The highly skilled athletes who take part in these sports are able to perform amazing, yet dangerous, moves that seem impossible to you and me! In this book you will read about all the top tricks and the most breathtaking extreme stunts. Who can jump the highest, who can fly through the air the farthest, and who can reach mind-blowing speeds. Check out these sports with our boarders and skaters, Oli, Laura, and Matt, and decide which sport YOU think offers the most EXTREME thrills.

GO FOR IT!

A group of skateboarders, skaters, and snowboarders were asked how often they take part in their sport. Here is a **bar graph** showing the results.

1) How many people do you **estimate** take part in their sport every day?

2) How many people do you estimate take part more than once a week?

3) Estimate the total number of people who take part in their sport *once a week* and *at least once a month*?

4) Which of these pieces of information can you find out from the bar graph?
   • The number of boys or girls taking part in extreme sports.
   • The number of 14-year-olds.
   • Which days of the week were most popular.
   • The total number of people questioned.

(You will find a TIP to help you with this activity on page 28.)

Number of skaters and boarders (y-axis: 5, 10, 15, 20, 25, 30, 35, 40, 45, 50, 55, 60, 65, 70, 75, 80, 85, 90, 95, 100, 105, 110, 115, 120, 125)

Categories: Every day / Several times a week / Once a week / At least once a month / Not at the moment – I'm injured

Backside boardslide down a handrail

MONEY FACT

Top professional skaters and boarders can win prize money in extreme sports competitions. Many **pros** are also paid by a company to endorse (use and promote) that company's products, such as skates, boards, clothes, shoes, hats, helmets, sunglasses, or goggles.

STREET SKATING FACT

Street skating is exactly what it says — using everyday obstacles that you see on the street to help you perform amazing tricks. Skateboarders and inline skaters ride off curbs, over park benches, and even down stairs and handrails!

VERT SKATING FACT

Vert skating is all about going up! "Vert" is short for *vertical*. Skateboarders and inline skaters perform flips, spins, grabs, and slides on ramps or in bowls and **halfpipes**. Vert skaters go to skateparks or build vert ramps.

Snowboarder Laura Berry rides a rainbow rail.

A "Japan air" on a halfpipe

CHALLENGE QUESTIONS

You are preparing for a snowboarding trip and need to choose a new board.

Snowboards come in different sizes to suit the rider's weight, ability, and style of riding.

Here are some snowboard designs. You will see the range of lengths each design comes in and the boards' prices.

Compare the different designs:

Board A
Length range: *55–61 in.*
Price: *$453*

Board B
Length range: *58–63 in.*
Price: *$529*

Board C
Length range: *59–62 in.*
Price: *$524*

Board D
Length range: *57–62 in.*
Price: *$519*

a) Which board offers the biggest **range** in length?
b) Which board costs $530 when rounded to the nearest ten dollars?

(You will find a TIP to help you with question b on page 28.)

SKATEBOARDING with Oli

Oli says, "Skateboarding is more than just a sport – there's a whole culture based around it, with companies dedicated to producing clothes, shoes, and videos for skateboarders. Skateboarding can give you an enormous sense of satisfaction, and it's also a great way to meet new people. Skateboarding is a very technical and skillful sport, and there are hundreds of tricks to learn. To be a good skateboarder, you need to be athletic and creative. The best skateboarders also have plenty of nerve and lots of dedication, because many top tricks can take years of practice to get right!"

GO FOR IT!

Here are three skateboard tricks.

What **fraction** of a whole turn has the skateboarder made in each trick, and how many **degrees** are there in the **angle** of the turn?

Trick 1)

Left foot   Right foot

Left foot   Right foot

Start position   *Finish position*

POWERSLIDES (tricks 1 and 2):
You shift your weight to one side of the board and slide the back wheels around into a sort of skid. This is a good way of slowing down.

Trick 2)

Start position   *Finish position*

SHOVE-IT (trick 3):
Do an *Ollie*, and while you are in the air, spin the board around underneath you.

Trick 3)

Head   Head

Tail   Tail

Start position   *Finish position*

(You will find TIPS to help you with these questions on page 28.)

SKATEBOARDING FACTS

The basis for most skateboarding tricks is the *Ollie*, which was invented in the late 1970s by Alan "Ollie" Gelfand. A skateboarder stomps on the tail of their board with their back foot. As the tail hits the ground, the skater hops up off that foot into the air — the board comes, too! The skater then pushes forward with their front foot, levels the board, and drops to the ground. Skateboarders can pull *Ollies* over three feet high, and it looks as though the board is actually stuck to their feet!

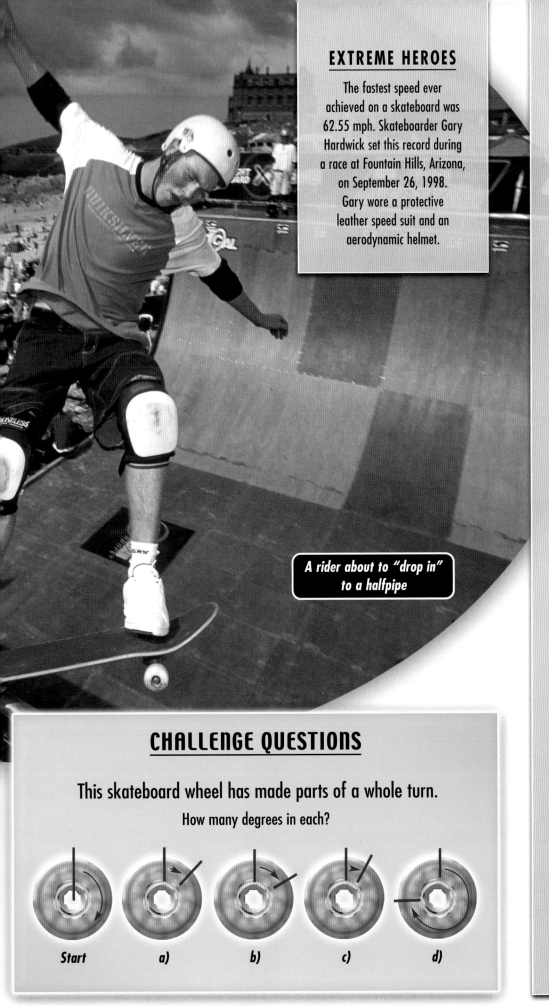

A rider about to "drop in" to a halfpipe

EXTREME HEROES

The fastest speed ever achieved on a skateboard was 62.55 mph. Skateboarder Gary Hardwick set this record during a race at Fountain Hills, Arizona, on September 26, 1998. Gary wore a protective leather speed suit and an aerodynamic helmet.

TRICK TALK

AIR "To air" is to jump into the air with a skateboard.

FAT (also *phat*) This describes a skateboarding trick that is performed over a long distance or to a great height.

FLIP When your board completely flips over and lands back on the wheels.

GOOFY If you skate or snowboard with your right foot forward.

KICKTURN Performed on a **halfpipe**, the skateboarder rotates on the rear wheels of the board with the front wheels raised up from the ground.

MANUAL Travelling on your board, balancing on just the rear wheels —a *wheelie*.

REGULAR If you skate or snowboard with your left foot forward.

REVERT Finishing a trick coming out forwards and then quickly sliding around 180 **degrees** to come out backwards.

SKETCHY When someone is wobbly and just about lands a trick, the trick is *sketchy*.

SLAM Falling off your skateboard and hurting yourself!

SWITCHSTANCE Skating or snowboarding in the opposite stance (regular or goofy) to the one you normally use.

CHALLENGE QUESTIONS

This skateboard wheel has made parts of a whole turn.

How many degrees in each?

Start   a)   b)   c)   d)

INLINE SKATING with Matt

Matt says, "Inline skating offers the **adrenaline** rush of high speeds and the thrill of performing tricks and stunts. Speed skaters hurtle around racetracks, while **aggressive skaters** perform jumps, spins, and grabs on street courses or vert ramps. *Aggressive skating* or *rolling* was started in the early 1990s by a group of extreme sports enthusiasts who each felt their current sport just didn't offer the kind of adrenaline rush they were looking for. Aggressive skating offers incredible thrills and it's also really convenient for beginners because the skates are attached to their feet, and so, unlike a skateboard, they can't go flying off during a trick!"

GO FOR IT!

Successful speed skaters combine high levels of fitness with good technique and tactics. In sprint races, groups of up to 10 skaters race to qualify for a final. It takes a lot of skill to skate at high speeds in close proximity to the other competitors.

A speed skater

In the final of a 330-yard sprint race there were 10 skaters. Use their times in the DATA BOX to answer these questions:

1) How many skaters had a time under 26 seconds?
2) Which skaters had a time over 27 seconds?
3) If another skater finished the sprint in 25.3 seconds, where would he be ranked – 3rd, 11th, or 5th?
4) Three racetracks are holding qualifying races in the first round of a speed skating competition.

- At TRACK A, 209 skaters have entered.
- At TRACK B, 92 skaters have entered.
- At TRACK C, 165 skaters have entered.

If there is a maximum of 10 skaters in a race, how many first-round qualifying races will there be at each location?

(You will find some information about PUTTING NUMBERS IN ORDER on page 28.)

SPEED SKATING FACT

Matt King has actually been caught speeding on his skates in London! In a daring stunt, performed on empty roads in the middle of the night, Matt and some friends actually managed to set off a speed camera. To build up their speed at the start of their run, the skaters held on to the back of a sports car. They were photographed by the speed camera travelling at 80 mph!

For a fast, fun night out, hundreds of inline skaters in cities, such as London, Paris, and New York, gather together to *night skate* and see the city. Marshals travel with the skaters to keep everyone under control.

DATA BOX
SPEED SKATER TIMES

NAME	TIME IN SECONDS
Jolly	25.0
Paul	24.4
Mo	25.2
Josh	27.9
Dec	25.6
Phil	26.3
Ant	30.2
Ian	24.7
Flo	26.8
Dave	31.5

An aggressive skater pulls a big "mute air" on a ramp.

TRICK TALK

AIRS can be performed both on street courses and vert ramps. While *airing*, skaters perform spins, flips, and grabs (grabbing their skates).

FLY FISH The right hand grabs the right boot and extends the leg, while the left foot stays tucked under the body.

MUTE AIR With the legs tucked up in front of the body, the skater reaches their right hand over both shins to grab the left boot.

ROCKET AIR Both legs are extended out in front of the body. The left hand reaches to touch the right toe, or right hand to left toe.

SAFETY GRAB Knees are tucked up so the body is in a ball, right hand on right boot, or left hand on left boot.

LUI KANG Knees to chest, left hand to left foot or right hand to right foot, then the free leg kicks out.

SKATE TALK

FACE PLANT or BAILS When your nose hits the sidewalk before your hands!

RASPBERRY The *road rash* you get when your skin scrapes the road or sidewalk.

CHALLENGE QUESTION

An aggressive skater pulls an *air* on a **halfpipe** and reaches a height of 4 meters.

What is this height approximately in feet?
5 feet   13 feet   23 feet

(You will find a TIP to help you with this question on page 28.)

L aura says, "Snowboarding is exciting, fun, and gives me a buzz! I get the chance to travel all over the world, meet new people, and make new friends. As long as everybody is having fun, snowboarders of all abilities will ride together, offering each other encouragement and helping each other progress and improve. I personally love to ride anywhere that has *big air jumps, superpipes,* and technical rails. Snowboarding competitions can take place on mountains, at indoor snow slopes, and on dry slopes. There are lots of different types of snowboarding competitions – *Pipe, Big Air, Snowboarder-cross,* and *Slopestyle.*"

GO FOR IT!

It is the final of a *halfpipe competition.* **Halfpipes** are like a giant pipe that has been cut in half. They are made of snow. Snowboarders ride down the pipe performing tricks. They are awarded points out of 10 in four categories. The rider with the highest total score is the winner.

In the DATA BOX you will see the scores for six halfpipe finalists.

1) Who got the lowest total score?
2) Who did better than Rob in both **amplitude** and overall impression?
3) Who got the same score as Zak?
4) How many people had total scores that were odd numbers? What were their scores?
5) Who got the highest score and won the halfpipe competition?

(You will find TIPS to help you with these questions on page 28.)

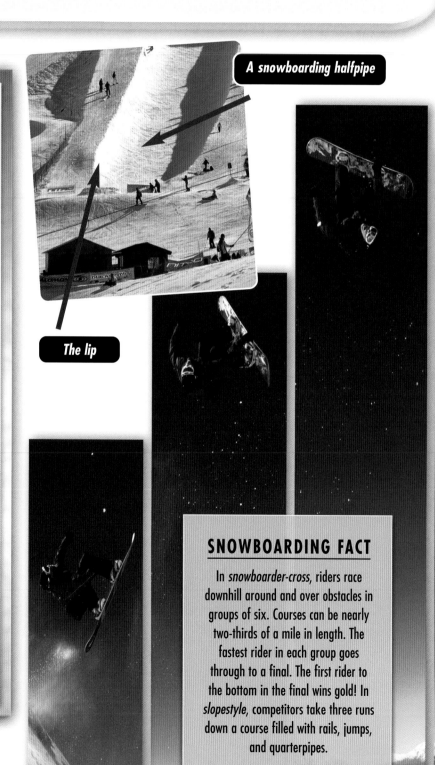

A snowboarding halfpipe

The lip

SNOWBOARDING FACT

In *snowboarder-cross,* riders race downhill around and over obstacles in groups of six. Courses can be nearly two-thirds of a mile in length. The fastest rider in each group goes through to a final. The first rider to the bottom in the final wins gold! In *slopestyle,* competitors take three runs down a course filled with rails, jumps, and quarterpipes.

DATA BOX HALFPIPE SCORES (POINTS OUT OF 40)

NAME	STANDARD AIRS	ROTATIONS	AMPLITUDE	OVERALL IMPRESSION
Lyn	5	9	8	4
Rob	8	8	7	8
Ahmed	6	9	6	9
Laura	9	8	8	7
Zak	7	7	8	9
Alli	8	5	5	5

- *STANDARD AIRS*: Tricks and movements such as grabs.
- *ROTATIONS* (spins and flips): 180°, 360° (a full spin), 540°, 720°, 900°, 1080°, 1260°.
- *AMPLITUDE*: The height the rider reaches above the lip of the pipe.
- *OVERALL IMPRESSION*: Style, level of difficulty of tricks, creativity, and landings.

SNOWBOARDING FACT

The highest *big air* ever achieved was 30 feet above the lip of the halfpipe. The biggest spin that has ever been done on a jump is a *1260* (that's 1,260 **degrees** — three and a half full spins while in the air).

CHALLENGE QUESTIONS

In *Big Air competitions*, riders perform big jumps.
They launch themselves out of a halfpipe and pull a trick.
Competitors are marked on height, style, and number of rotations.

This graph shows the amplitude (height) of some snowboarders' *big air jumps*.

a) What was the **range** of heights jumped?

b) Can you find the *mode* (the most common height of jump)?

(You will find a TIP to help you with these questions on page 28.)

PRACTICE MAKES PERFECT

Many top extreme athletes actually turned professional while they were still at school, and they are now able to make a living from their sport. However, to keep their places at the top, some professionals practice for up to eight hours every day! Oli, Laura, and Matt all agree that the only way to get to grips with all the most impressive tricks and jumps is to practice, practice, and then practice again. If you want to be the best, the only way is to put the hours in. Of course, if you love your sport, the more time you can spend on your board or skates, the better!

GO FOR IT!

Here is a **pictograph** showing the number of times some tricks were attempted by a skateboarder, an inline skater, and a snowboarder during one week.

TRICKS

SKATEBOARDER

a) *Kickflip*

b) *50-50 grind*

c) *Ollie*

⬤ = 10 times

◉ = 10 times

❄ = 10 times

INLINE SKATER

a) *Mute air*

b) *Lui Kang*

c) *Safety grab*

SNOWBOARDER

a) *Rodeo*

b) *Frontside 540 melon*

c) *Backside 180 Indy*

1) How many times was trick *a* practiced in each sport?
2) How many more times was trick *a* practiced than trick *b* in each sport?
3) How many times did each extreme sportsperson practice all their tricks?

Check out TRICK TALK on page 32 for more information on these tricks.

(You will find information about PICTOGRAPHS on page 28.)

EXTREME HEROES

Matt says, "Shane (Tasmanian Devil) Yost is a professional inline skater famous for his flips and spins. Shane was the first skater to pull a *1260* (that's 1,260 degrees — three and a half full spins in midair)."

EXTREME HEROES

Laura says, "Snowboarder Jussi Oksanen from Finland is fast becoming a hero to snowboarders everywhere. Jussi has a great style and he can spin *1080s* (that's 1,080 **degrees** — three full spins) in both switchstance and his normal stance."

EXTREME HEROES

Oli says, "Tony Hawk is one of the world's most famous skateboarders. He has won hundreds of competitions and invented dozens of tricks. He turned professional when he was just 14 years old. Tony went into skateboarding history when he landed the first ever *900* (that's 900 degrees — two and a half midair turns) at the 1999 *X Games*."

Tony Hawk pulls a "gymnast plant."

Laura Berry performing a "frontside 540 melon."

CHALLENGE QUESTIONS

How long do skates and boards last? Oli says, "A skateboard belonging to a beginner could last for a year. But a board belonging to a **pro**, who is practicing jumping down a set of 20 steps, might only last for an hour!"

These boards and skates have all been used for hours of tough practicing. They are now worn out or damaged, and are no longer in use.

The inline skate wheels lasted: May and June

The snowboard lasted: 336 hours

The skateboard lasted: 10,080 minutes

a) How long did each last in days?
b) How long did each last in weeks?

(You will find a TIP to help you with these questions on page 28.)

STREET COMPETITIONS

Skateboarders and **aggressive skaters** get to showcase their talents in *street comp etitions*. The skaters compete on courses made up of boxes, quarterpipes, and rails. The obstacles on the courses are made to look and feel like the steps, curbs, hills, and railings that the skaters would use on the street. Each skater usually gets 45 seconds to one minute to move around the course. The competitors must use as many of the different obstacles as possible to perform their tricks. There are no compulsories (moves that the competitors have to do). The competition judges look for creativity, style, level of difficulty of tricks, and the overall flow of the skater's run.

GO FOR IT!

In *street competitions*, five or six judges award points to each skater. The lowest and highest marks are thrown out, and the remaining marks are averaged. The skater with the highest score out of 100 wins the competition.

On these pages you will see some routes that skateboarders and aggressive skaters took across a street course. Each route starts with 100 points (the maximum points a skater can earn in a competition). Along the route you will see all the judges' calculations. Follow each of the routes and do the calculations as you go along.

What is the skater's final score at the end of each route?

START

100

−95   ÷5

x10   x7

÷2   +60

÷5   +35   ÷100   ÷20

+75   ÷3   +7   x11

÷4   −10   x10   −99

ROUTE 1   ROUTE 2   ROUTE 3   ROUTE 4

EXTREME HEROES

In 2002, skateboarder Danny Way set a record for the *longest air*. He dropped down a 49-foot roll-in into a jump ramp, took off, and flew an incredible 65 feet, landing safely on a landing ramp. The next day, Danny set a *high air* record of 18.24 feet off a quarterpipe. Danny actually broke his neck in a surfing accident, but he recovered to continue with his amazing skateboarding career.

A "royale" down a stair handrail

A skateboarder pulls a "melancholy grab" on a street course.

x2

−50

÷2

+15   ÷5

double it   x10

÷10   ÷3

ROUTE 5   **ROUTE 6**

CHALLENGE QUESTION

100 skateboarders were asked how often they bought a new deck. Here are the results:

Once a month	27
Once every three months	30
Once every six months	23
Once every year	20

If the skateboards came from one shop, how many skateboards would be sold in one year to these skateboarders?

The average size of a skateboard deck is 3 to 8.5 in. wide, 32 in. long, and 0.4 in. thick.

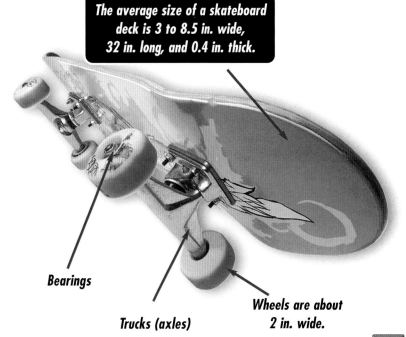

Bearings

Trucks (axles)

Wheels are about 2 in. wide.

NEED FOR SPEED

n speed skating competitions, inline skaters compete on flat or banked tracks and on roads that are closed specially for the race. Top speed skaters compete in championship competitions, while skaters of all abilities can take part in *rat races*. During a race, skaters form pace lines (groups), where the competitors take turns to **slipstream** each other to conserve energy. Depending on their tactics, skaters will move from group to group, slowing down, then speeding up again throughout the race. As the end of the race approaches, the skaters will break from their groups, make their final moves, and sprint for the finish line.

GO FOR IT!

Speed skaters compete over a variety of distances, from 328-yard sprint races to 31-mile marathons and 100-mile endurance races.

A speed skating competition is being held on a track that is 130 yards long.
The speed skaters will compete in races of these distances:

a) 500 yd.   b) 1,000 yd.   c) 1,500 yd.   d) 5,000 yd.

1) Match these numbers of laps to the races above:

e) More than 11, but less than 12
f) More than 3, but less than 4
g) More than 38, but less than 39
h) More than 7, but less than 8

2) Which of the four races is closest to an exact number of laps?

Some races are being held on a track that is 400 yards long.

3. How many laps and **fractions** of a lap do competitors cover in the following races:

a) 500 yd.   b) 1,000 yd.   c) 1,500 yd.
d) 3,000 yd.   e) 5,000 yd.   f) 10,000 yd.

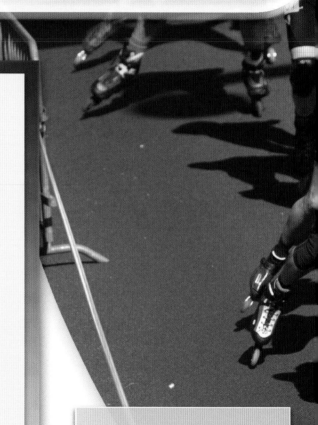

EXTREME HEROES

In September 2003, inline skater Jürgen Köhler set a new world inline speed record of 174.75 miles per hour. How did he do it? By wearing custom-built speed skates, worth $12,850, and by holding on to a Suzuki Hayabusa motorbike! Köhler had to make a number of attempts at reaching his record-breaking speed, and at one point, the Hayabusa actually caught fire! However, after a hard day's skating, a new record was achieved.

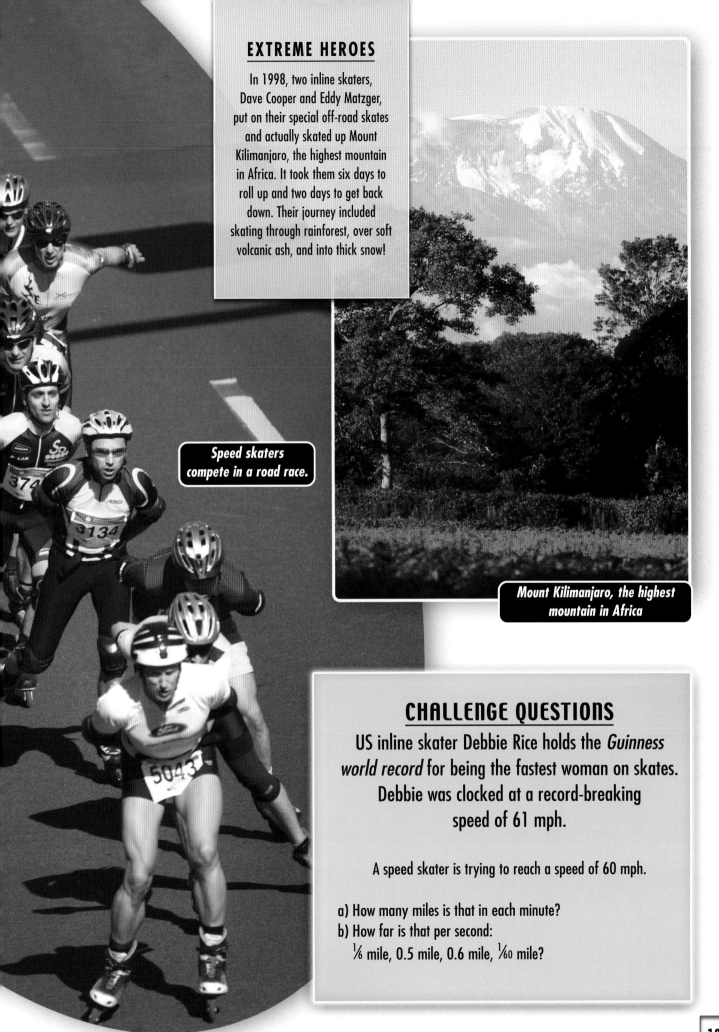

EXTREME HEROES

In 1998, two inline skaters, Dave Cooper and Eddy Matzger, put on their special off-road skates and actually skated up Mount Kilimanjaro, the highest mountain in Africa. It took them six days to roll up and two days to get back down. Their journey included skating through rainforest, over soft volcanic ash, and into thick snow!

Speed skaters compete in a road race.

Mount Kilimanjaro, the highest mountain in Africa

CHALLENGE QUESTIONS

US inline skater Debbie Rice holds the *Guinness world record* for being the fastest woman on skates. Debbie was clocked at a record-breaking speed of 61 mph.

A speed skater is trying to reach a speed of 60 mph.

a) How many miles is that in each minute?
b) How far is that per second:
$\frac{1}{6}$ mile, 0.5 mile, 0.6 mile, $\frac{1}{60}$ mile?

Sometimes only the highest, most dangerous slopes will do. In May 2001, 22-year-old Marco Siffredi became the first person to snowboard down Mount Everest, the world's highest mountain peak. Marco and his support team climbed to the summit of Everest and then, at first light, Marco set off alone on his amazing downward journey. It took Marco just two and a half hours to snowboard down Everest. He used no special equipment, just his snowboard and his own tremendous skill and nerve. Sadly, some months later, while attempting to repeat this snowboarding feat, Marco disappeared. A sad end to an amazing extreme sports story.

GO FOR IT!

See if you can conquer these questions about extreme slopes and the world's highest mountains.

1) If Marco Siffredi snowboarded 8,000 yards in 2 hours, how far did he snowboard in 1 hour?

2) At how many miles per hour did Marco travel?

3) Find the difference in heights between the megamountains in the DATA BOX:

a) Mount McKinley and Vinson Massif
b) Everest and Aconcagua
c) Kilimanjaro and Elbrus
d) Aconcagua and Vinson Massif
e) Everest and Kilimanjaro

(You will find a TIP to help you with question 3 on page 29.)

SNOWBOARD TALK

CARVE To weave back and forth, while going downhill.

WIND LIPS Natural jumps made from snow, blown into place by the wind.

HIT When a snowboarder pulls a trick in the air.

SNOWBOARDING FACT

In some of the world's most extreme places, such as Alaska, it is so difficult to get to the slopes that snowboarders have to be dropped on the mountain tops by helicopters.

Here are some of the world's highest mountains. All of these mountains have been conquered by snowboarders!

| Asia: Mount Everest 29,035 feet high | South America: Aconcagua 22,835 feet high | North America: Mount McKinley 20,322 feet high | Africa: Kilimanjaro 19,341 feet high | Europe: Elbrus 18,511 feet high | Antarctica: Vinson Massif 16,066 feet high |

An extreme snowboarder riding off-piste.

CHALLENGE QUESTION

Snowboarding trails (routes that can be taken down a mountain) are given different ratings according to their level of difficulty. Snowboarders need to watch out for these symbols.

The snowboard trail symbols are all symmetrical.

EASIEST RUN

MORE DIFFICULT

DIFFICULT

VERY DIFFICULT – use extreme caution

The green circle has an infinite number of **lines of symmetry**. How many lines of symmetry do the other two symbols have?

(You will find information about LINES OF SYMMETRY on page 29.)

SNOWBOARDING FACT

Snowboarders have been killed by **avalanches**. When riding **off-piste**, snowboarders need to check the snow conditions to make sure there is no danger of an avalanche. They often carry small devices called transceivers. If snowboarders become trapped under an avalanche, the transceiver will give out a signal that can help rescuers find them.

In *vert competitions* skaters and skateboarders show what they can do on ramps, **halfpipes,** and boxes (huge plywood boxes with sloping sides). Skaters are not disqualified if they fall because it's all about going for the most difficult and exciting moves. The story goes that **vert skating** was invented one summer completely by accident. A young skateboarder drained his family's swimming pool so that he and his friends could roll down towards the deep end on their skateboards. The skaters soon realized that with enough speed they could actually ride up the walls of the swimming pool. A whole new range of skating possibilities opened up!

GO FOR IT!

Many skaters and skateboarders actually build ramps and boxes so that they can create skateparks in their own gardens!

A group of skaters have been busy building a ramp from plywood. Some pieces have been sorted into groups according to shape. One of the groups contains the shapes shown below the overlapping circles.

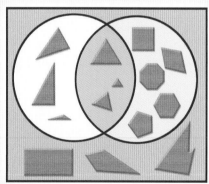

1) How have the shapes been sorted?

2) How many triangles can you find here?

(You will find a TIP to help you with question 1 on page 29.)

Skaters wait on the platform to "drop in."

CIRCUIT CITY

Vert area – this section goes straight up.

EXTREME HEROES

UK skateboarders Joel and Paul Spaven and Jamie Manby have built the world's longest skateboard. The giant board is 23.65 feet long, 11.81 inches wide, and 2.95 inches thick. It cost $750 to build.

Transition

A COMPETITION HALFPIPE WOULD BE:

Overall length: 46 feet
Overall width: 16 feet
Vertical height: 11.5 feet
Flat area between transitions: 16 feet

VERT SKATING TALK

HALFPIPE A U-shaped ramp with a flat section in the middle. When viewed from the side, it looks like a giant pipe cut in half. The vertical, or *vert*, area at the top stops the skaters drifting away from the ramp when they launch into air tricks.

MINIRAMP A small halfpipe 3 to 6 feet high, but with no *vert* area.

QUARTERPIPE One half of a miniramp or a quarter of a pipe if viewed from the side. Quarterpipes are usually found in the street area at skateparks.

BOWLS Giant bowl-shaped areas in the ground. Bowls are normally found at outdoor parks and are made from concrete.

A tail grab

CHALLENGE QUESTIONS

Here are the plans for a ramp. The plans show the length, width, and height of the ramp.

a) What is the **area** of the ramp's surface approximately?
b) What is the **perimeter** of the ramp's surface approximately?

70 in.

23 in.

49 in.

(You will find TIPS to help you with these questions on page 29.)

Flat area

Lip, or coping – a metal edge that can be used

CIRCUIT CITY.

AT THE EXTREME SPORTS CENTER

O li and Matt say, "**Street skating** is now illegal in a lot of public places. Many towns and cities around the world have passed laws that ban this type of skating because it can cause damage to railings, curbs, steps, and park benches. Skateparks offer a safe and legal way for skaters and skateboarders to enjoy their sport without getting into trouble! They are also a great place to show off all your best moves and meet up with your friends." Laura says, "Indoor snowboarding facilities mean snowboarders can ride and practice their tricks all year round – even if it's hot and sunny outside."

GO FOR IT!

A new extreme sports center has just opened. Some skaters and boarders are checking out the equipment shop and snack bar.

1) Tickets to get into the new center cost $9. With $57, how many tickets could you buy?

2) A meal in the snack bar is $5.99. How many meals can be bought with $30?

3) Tubes of *shoe goo* are packed in boxes of 70 tubes. If ⅖ of a box is sold, how many tubes are left? If 214 tubes are sold, how many boxes will need to be opened?

4. There are 506 pairs of knee pads in stock, 52 of which are on display. Half of the knee pads not on display are sent to another sports center shop. How many pairs is that?

5. Badges are displayed on cards. There are 60 badges on each card. How many rows of badges will there be on a card if the badges are arranged in rows of **10, 5, 20, 3, 12?**

(You will find a TIP to help you with question 2 on page 29.)

SKATE TALK

JAM Getting a load of **aggressive skaters** or skateboarders together for a skating *session*.

SESSION The act of skateboarding or inline skating. For example, you can *session a ramp* or *have a street session*.

THRASHED or WRECKED The wear and tear on an object due to skateboarding or skating.

WALLIE Skating onto, up, and over a street object.

WALLRIDE Skating up a vertical wall.

STOKED The feeling of doing something well.

24

SNOWBOARDING FACT

Snowboarding as we know it today was started in 1965. A guy called Sherman Poppen, from Michigan, screwed two skis together to create, what he called, a *snurfer*. He created this name from the words *snow* and *surfer*.

GEAR GUIDE

IMPACT SHORTS Snowboarders often wear these to provide protection for their hips and lower back. The shorts contain thick padding.

SHOES Skateboarding can cause some serious wear and tear on your shoes. You can buy special skateboarding shoes with ultrathick rubber soles or use *shoe goo* on your regular sneakers.

SHOE GOO This liquid rubber can be put over holes in your shoes or used to rebuild the soles. Spread it on and watch it harden!

SKATE JEANS Wide and baggy jeans that give you plenty of room for your knee and shin pads. The bottoms are wide enough to drop over your skates. The jeans can contain removable padding.

CHALLENGE QUESTIONS

A survey is done during the first hour that the new extreme sports center is open. The results are entered on a *tally chart*.

LOCATION IN THE CENTER	NUMBER OF PEOPLE
Spectator area	⳾⳾⳾ ⳾⳾⳾ ⳾⳾⳾ ⳾⳾⳾ ⳾⳾⳾ II
Snowboarding area	⳾⳾⳾ ⳾⳾⳾ ⳾⳾⳾ ⳾⳾⳾ ⳾⳾⳾ ⳾⳾⳾ ⳾⳾⳾ III
Street course	⳾⳾⳾ ⳾⳾⳾ ⳾⳾⳾ ⳾⳾⳾ ⳾⳾⳾ ⳾⳾⳾ ⳾⳾⳾ ⳾⳾⳾ ⳾⳾⳾ ⳾⳾⳾ I
Vert ramps	⳾⳾⳾ ⳾⳾⳾ ⳾⳾⳾ IIII
Snack bar	⳾⳾⳾ ⳾⳾⳾ ⳾⳾⳾ ⳾⳾⳾ ⳾⳾⳾ II
Equipment shop	⳾⳾⳾ ⳾⳾⳾ ⳾⳾⳾ ⳾⳾⳾
Amusement arcade	⳾⳾⳾ ⳾⳾⳾ I

a) Which facility is least popular?

b) What is the difference in the number of people who are snowboarding compared with those who are **vert skating**?

c) How many people are taking part in extreme sports altogether?

d) If 15 more people go for a snack, what will the new snack bar total be?

(You will find information about TALLY CHARTS on page 29.)

Laura Berry rides a rail at an indoor snowboarding center.

The world's top extreme athletes get plenty of chances to meet up and compete against each other. Snowboarders compete in the Winter Olympics, and skaters and skateboarders take part in competitions such as the *X Games* and the *Gravity Games*. At the *X Games*, the winning skaters take home cash prizes and medals. Skating and boarding companies usually have a team of around ten or twenty boarders or skaters who, as part of their deal with the company, take part in competitions and demonstrations around the world. On these pages you will see snowboarders, skaters, and skateboarders who are showcasing their skills in the EXTREME SPORTS CHALLENGE.

GO FOR IT!

Each of the competitors is working hard to impress the crowds and grab the judges' attention!

1) The most steps a skateboarder has cleared so far today is seven. Jez takes off and clears three times that many. How many steps has Jez jumped?

2) Ed is trying to land a *900*. He falls 9 times, but lands the trick 3 times. Show Ed's successes as a **fraction** of his tota number of attempts. Then show your answer as a **decimal fraction**.

3) Cal has just achieved an **amplitude** of 324 inches in the *Big Air competition*. How much higher does he need to jump to reach the *highest air* record of 30 feet?

4) Charlie has been awarded the following points on her street run: 44, 15, 9, and 28. Use Charlie's scores to make as many addition and subtraction statements as you can.

Judges in sports competitions need to be able to order numbers.

5) Can you place these decimal fractions where they go on the number line?   0.7, 0.2, 1.3, 1.9, 0.6, 1.5, 1.1, 0.8

(You will find information about NUMBER LINES on page 29.)

SKATEBOARDING FACT

Street luge is STRICTLY for the **pros**. Riders lay flat on their backs on special extralong skateboards. They hurtle downhill on twisting, turning courses at speeds of up to 70 mph. Street lugers wear full-body leather suits and motorcycle helmets. They also wear rubber-soled shoes because they use their feet to brake!

SNOWBOARDING FACT

Snowboarding became an official Olympic sport in 1998, when it was included in the Winter Olympics at Nagano in Japan.

Charlie

Cal

Ed

Matt

Laura

CHALLENGE QUESTIONS

Snow sports need low temperatures. When it gets below zero degrees, we use negative numbers on the Fahrenheit scale. Look at the thermometer:

10°F

0°F

−10°F

a) The temperature rises by 5 **degrees**. What is the new temperature?

b) If the temperature is −5°F and rises to 8°F, how much warmer has it become?

c) The temperature starts out at zero degrees. It rises 9° during the day and then drops 11° at night. What is the nighttime temperature?

GO FOR IT!

Interpreting a bar graph:

Bar graphs have bars that should always be the same width. It is the heights of the bars that allow you to compare things. In a bar graph, you need to know what each bar stands for and what the scale is. *For example, is the scale going up in 1s, 2s, 5s, 10s, 100s, 1,000s, or some other amount?*

CHALLENGE QUESTIONS

Rounding whole numbers and decimal fractions:

When rounding whole numbers and **decimal fractions**, we always follow the same rules:
36 rounded to the nearest ten is 40 because we round up numbers that end in 5, 6, 7, 8, or 9. We round down numbers that end in 4, 3, 2, or 1.
For example, 32 would be rounded down to 30.
When rounding decimal fractions to the nearest whole number, we use the same rules:
so 3.6 is rounded up to 4 and 3.2 is rounded down to 3.

Making and measuring angles:

An **angle** is a shape formed when two line segments share the same endpoint. The center of a circle is the shared endpoint. Angles are measured in degrees. The symbol for degrees is °. The line segments in a 90° angle make a quarter-turn around a circle. A 90° angle is called a right angle. There are four right angles in 360°, one complete turn.

GO FOR IT!

Ordering numbers:

When we put things in order 1st, 2nd, 3rd, 4th, and so on, we are using *ordinal numbers*. When we count 1, 2, 3, 4, and so on, we use *cardinal numbers*.

CHALLENGE QUESTION

TIP: One foot is about 30 centimeters.

GO FOR IT!

TIPS: When adding several small numbers:
- See if you can begin with the largest number.
- Look for pairs to make ten.
- Find numbers appearing more than once so that you can use multiplication tables.

For example, 7 + 7 + 7 is the same as 3 x 7.

CHALLENGE QUESTION

Interpreting a bar graph:

The graph in this section is known as a *bar graph*. Use a ruler or pencil to check and compare the heights of the bars in the graph.

Sometimes we can connect the tops of the lines in a bar graph to make a continuous graph. The tops of the bars here cannot be joined because the bits of information are separate from one another. Joining one person's *big air jump* height to another's makes no sense.

GO FOR IT!

Using data in a pictograph:

A **pictograph** is a chart where a picture is used to show several units. In the pictograph on page 14, a picture of a complete wheel or snowflake stands for practicing a trick 10 times. Pictures can be cut into **fractions** so each of these half-pictures show 5 times.

CHALLENGE QUESTIONS

TIP: There are —
- 60 minutes in one hour.
- 24 hours in one day.
- 7 days in one week.
- 4–5 weeks in one month.

You can use a calendar to find out exactly how many days there are in each of the 12 months of the year.

PAGES 20–21

GO FOR IT!

Writing down calculations:

When working with large numbers, you can write the problem on paper to make it easier to figure out the answer. Remember to line up the numbers so that the thousands go under the thousands and so on. Look at these examples:

$$2,285 \qquad\qquad 9,785$$
$$+4,193 \qquad\qquad -2,315$$
$$6,478 \qquad\qquad 7,470$$

CHALLENGE QUESTION

TIP: If a shape can be cut in half so that the halves match, we say that it has a **line of symmetry**. Wherever you cut a circle, as long as you go through the center, your cut will be along a line of symmetry.

PAGES 22–23

GO FOR IT!

Using Venn diagrams to display information about shapes:

This type of diagram is called a *Venn diagram*. In this example, the sets of shapes intersect (overlap).

TIP: **2-D** shapes with three or more sides are called *polygons*. A regular 2-D shape has all sides the same length.

CHALLENGE QUESTIONS

Measuring the area and perimeter of rectangles:
TIP: To find the **area** of a rectangle you need to multiply the length by the width.

10 in.

5 in.   5 in.

10 in.

The area of this rectangle is 50 square in. (or 50 in.²). To find the **perimeter** you add all the sides. So the perimeter of this rectangle is 30 in.

PAGES 24–25

GO FOR IT!

TIP: When doing money calculations, you can round up prices to figure out approximate amounts. For example, $5.99 can be rounded to $6, which makes it easier to do the math in your head. Don't forget to subtract 1¢ from the answer at the end.

CHALLENGE QUESTIONS

Using data in a tally chart:

A *tally chart* is a quick way of recording or counting the amount of something. One of something is shown as one *tally mark* "I." The fifth line is drawn across the first four (IIII) to make five lines in total. Use your knowledge of the products of the 5x table to quickly add when using *tally marks*.

PAGES 26–27

GO FOR IT!

Number lines:
A number line is continuous and extends forever in both directions.

$$-5 \quad -4 \quad -3 \quad -2 \quad -1 \quad 0 \quad 1 \quad 2 \quad 3 \quad 4 \quad 5$$

UNITS OF MEASUREMENT

There are two systems of measurement. The customary system uses inches, feet, miles, ounces, and pounds. The metric system uses centimeters, meters, kilometers, grams, and kilograms.

METRIC		CUSTOMARY	
Length		**Length**	
1 millimeter (mm)		1 inch (in.)	
1 centimeter (cm)	= 10 mm	1 foot (ft.)	= 12 in.
1 meter (m)	= 100 cm	1 yard (yd.)	= 3 ft.
1 kilometer (km)	= 1,000 m	1 mile	= 1,760 yd.
Weight		**Weight**	
1 gram (g)		1 ounce (oz.)	
1 kilogram (kg)	= 1,000 g	1 pound (lb.)	= 16 oz.
Capacity		**Capacity**	
1 milliliter (ml)		1 fluid ounce (fl. oz.)	
1 liter (l)	= 1,000 ml	1 pint (pt.)	= 16 fl. oz.

Comparing metric and customary measurements:

1 kilometer = 0.62 of a mile   1 kilogram = 2.2 pounds
0.47 liter = 1 pint

GO FOR IT!

1) Slightly more than 120 (122)
2) About 200 people
3) Slightly more than 10 + 5 (12 + 5 = 17)
4) The total number of people questioned can be found out from the **bar graph**.

CHALLENGE QUESTIONS

a) Board A offers the biggest **range**: 6 in.
b) Board B is $530 when rounded to the nearest ten dollars.

GO FOR IT!

Trick 1) The skateboarder made a ¼ turn, which is 90°.
Trick 2) The skateboarder made a ½ turn, which is 180°.
Trick 3) The skateboarder made a whole turn, which is 360°.

CHALLENGE QUESTIONS

a) 45°   b) 60°   c) 30°   d) 270°

GO FOR IT!

1) 5 skaters had a time under 26 seconds.
2) Josh, Ant, and Dave had a time over 27 seconds.
3) If another skater finished the sprint in 25.3 seconds, he would be ranked 5th.
4) • At TRACK A there will be 21 races.
   • At TRACK B there will be 10 races.
   • At TRACK C there will be 17 races.

CHALLENGE QUESTION

The height of the jump is approximately 13 feet.

GO FOR IT!

1) Alli got the lowest total score.
2) Zak did better than Rob in both **amplitude** and overall impression.
3) Rob got the same score as Zak.
4) Three people — Rob (31), Zak (31), and Alli (23)
5) Laura won the competition with 32 points.

CHALLENGE QUESTIONS

a) The **range** of heights jumped was 9 feet.
b) The *mode* (most common height of jump) was 16 feet.

GO FOR IT!

1) Trick a was practiced:
   SKATEBOARDER: *Kickflip* 40 times
   INLINE SKATER: *Mute air* 60 times
   SNOWBOARDER: *Rodeo* 100 times

2) SKATEBOARDER: *Kickflips* were practiced 15 more times than *50-50 grinds*.
   INLINE SKATER: *Mute airs* were practiced 10 more times than *Lui Kangs*.
   SNOWBOARDER: *Rodeos* were practiced 35 more times than *frontside 540 melons*.

3) SKATEBOARDER: 135 times
   INLINE SKATER: 175 times
   SNOWBOARDER: 180 times

CHALLENGE QUESTIONS

a) • The inline skate wheels lasted 61 days.
   • The snowboard lasted 14 days.
   • The skateboard lasted 7 days (168 hours).
b) • The inline skate wheels lasted 8 weeks and 5 days.
   • The snowboard lasted 2 weeks.
   • The skateboard lasted 1 week.

PAGES 16–17

GO FOR IT!

Route 1:	20	Route 2:	10
Route 3:	90	Route 4:	11
Route 5:	18	Route 6:	50

CHALLENGE QUESTION

The shop would sell 510 skateboards.

PAGES 18–19

GO FOR IT!

1) e and c / f and a / g and d/ h and b
2) Race a 500 yd. (race a is just under 4 laps, race b is just over 7½ laps, races c and d are nearly 11½ and 38½ laps respectively)
3) a) 1¼ laps b) 2½ laps c) 3¾ laps
    d) 7½ laps e) 12½ laps f) 25 laps

CHALLENGE QUESTIONS

a) 1 mile in each minute
b) ⅟₆₀ mile per second

PAGES 20–21

GO FOR IT!

1) 4,000 yards
2) 4,000 yd. per hour

3)
a) McKinley and Vinson Massif
$$20,322 - 16,066 = 4,256 \text{ feet}$$

b) Everest and Aconcagua
$$29,035 - 22,835 = 6,200 \text{ feet}$$

c) Kilimanjaro and Elbrus
$$19,341 - 18,511 = 830 \text{ feet}$$

d) Aconcagua and Vinson Massif
$$22,835 - 16,066 = 6,769 \text{ feet}$$

e) Everest and Kilimanjaro
$$29,035 - 19,341 = 9,694 \text{ feet}$$

CHALLENGE QUESTION

A square has **4 lines of symmetry**.

A rhombus has 2 lines of symmetry.

PAGES 22–23

GO FOR IT!

1) The pieces were sorted into the following sets:

Triangles

Triangles that are regular polygons

Regular polygons

Shapes that are neither regular or triangles

2) You can find 10 triangles:

CHALLENGE QUESTIONS

a) 24 square feet (24 ft.²) approximately
b) 20 feet approximately

PAGES 24–25

GO FOR IT!

1) 6 tickets   2) 5 meals
3) 50 tubes, 4 boxes   4) 227 pairs of knee pads
5) 6, 12, 3, 20, 5

CHALLENGE QUESTIONS

a) The amusement arcade is the least popular.
b) The difference is 19.
c) 108 people are taking part in extreme sports altogether.
d) The new snack bar total will be 42.

PAGES 26–27

GO FOR IT!

1) 21 steps   2) ¼ or 0.25
3) 36 inches
4) You can make lots of statements. For example,
   $44 - 28 = 16, \ 9 + 15 = 24, \ 44 + 9 + 15 = 68$
5)   A: 0.2 B: 0.6 C: 0.7 D: 0.8
       E: 1.1 F: 1.3 G: 1.5 H: 1.9

CHALLENGE QUESTIONS

a) 4° F   b) 13 **degrees** warmer   c) − 2° F

GLOSSARY

ADRENALINE A chemical produced in your body. It increases your heart rate and blood pressure, making you feel a rush of excitement or fear.

AGGRESSIVE SKATERS Inline skaters who perform tricks, such as airs, spins, flips, and grabs, on ramps and pipes or over street obstacles.

AMPLITUDE The height a snowboarder jumps above the lip of a halfpipe.

AVALANCHES Large masses of snow that break loose and move down the side of a mountain.

BACKSIDE Moving or jumping with your back facing the direction you are travelling in. The opposite to *frontside*.

HALFPIPES U-shaped ramps (normally made from wood) that when viewed from the side look like giant pipes cut in half. Skateboarders and inline skaters use them for vert skating. In snowboarding, halfpipes are like long pipes that have been cut in half. They are made of snow.

OFF-PISTE Snowboarding on a mountain slope that has not been prepared for skiing or snowboarding.

PROS (Professionals) Skaters, skateboarders, or snowboarders who are paid to take part in their sport.

SLIPSTREAM Using the stream of air created by the person in front of you to pull you along.

STREET SKATING Using everyday items such as curbs, park benches, stairs, and handrails to perform tricks.

VERT SKATING Using bowls, ramps, and halfpipes to perform tricks and gain height. "Vert" is short for *vertical*.

TRICK TALK

SKATEBOARDING

KICKFLIP While you are in the air, you kick down on the front of your board and spin it around underneath you.

50-50 GRIND Start parallel to an obstacle such as a curb or a rail. *Ollie* onto the obstacle so both trucks (axles) grind against it, then jump off.

BOARDSLIDE Like a grind, but your board is at 90° to the obstacle, with the middle of your board grinding along the obstacle.

SNOWBOARDING

RODEO You do a full back flip in the air while spinning 540°.

540 MELON One and a half spins, while grabbing the board between your legs at the back with your front hand.

BACKSIDE 180 INDY If you are goofy, you spin 180° counterclockwise, while grabbing the board with your back hand between your legs, at the front.

MATH GLOSSARY

2-D (TWO-DIMENSIONAL) Flat with length (or height) and width, but no depth (thickness).

ANGLE Shape formed when two line segments share the same endpoint. The center of a circle is the shared endpoint.

AREA The measure of the size of a surface, made in squares (all of the same size).

BAR GRAPH A graph with bars of the same width that can be used to compare numbers of things against a scale.

DECIMAL FRACTIONS We use a counting system involving tens, multiples of ten, and fractions of ten. The decimal point separates whole numbers from decimal fractions. *For example, in the number 672.53, 5 is tenths and 3 is hundredths.*

DEGREES The units used for measuring angles and temperatures.

ESTIMATE To find a number or amount that is close to an exact answer.

FRACTIONS These are made when shapes or numbers are cut into equal parts. For example, if a shape is cut into four equal parts, each part is one whole divided by four, or a quarter (¼).

LINE OF SYMMETRY A line dividing a shape into two matching halves.

PERIMETER The distance all the way around a shape.

PICTOGRAPH In a pictograph pictures are used to show information.

RANGE The difference between the highest and the lowest values.

t=top, b=bottom, c=center, l=left, r=right, OFC=outside front cover, OBC=outside back cover
Alamy: OFC, 2-3, 6cr, 7bl, 8-9, 10-11, 12, 14-15main, 17t, 17br, 18-19main, 20-21main, 24-25t, 26cr, 26-27c, 27tl, 27tr, 27cr, OBC.
Anna Bond (Matt King): 1. Corbis: 19tr. TheBoarder.co.uk: 6-7main, 15b, 27bl.
The Friedman Archives (Gary Friedman): 17c, 22-23. www.dopeshots.com: 24-25b.
Every effort has been made to trace the copyright holders, and we apologize in advance for any unintentional omissions.
We would be pleased to insert the appropriate acknowledgements in any subsequent edition of this publication.